GLE

THE STEA

Cardiff Libraries
www.cardiff.gov.uk/libraries

Llyfrgelloedd Caerdydd
www.caerdydd.gov.uk/llyfrgelloed

ACC. No: 05031710

With special thanks to Tabitha Jones

For Charlie David Manning

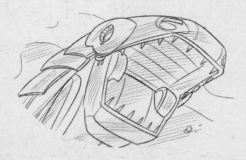

ORCHARD BOOKS

First published in Great Britain in 2016 by The Watts Publishing Group

1 3 5 7 9 10 8 6 4 2

Text © 2016 Beast Quest Limited.
Cover and inside illustrations by Artful Doodlers with special thanks to Bob and Justin
© Orchard Books 2016

Series created by Beast Quest Limited, London

The moral rights of the author and illustrator have been asserted.

All characters and events in this publication, other than those clearly in the public
domain, are fictitious and any resemblance to real persons, living or dead, is purely
coincidental.

All rights reserved.
No part of this publication may be reproduced, stored in a retrieval system, or
transmitted, in any form or by any means, without the prior permission in writing of the
publisher, nor be otherwise circulated in any form of binding or cover other than that
in which it is published and without a similar condition including this condition being
imposed on the subsequent purchaser.

A CIP catalogue record for this book is available from the British Library.

ISBN 978 1 40834 066 0

Printed in Great Britain

MIX
Paper from
responsible sources
FSC® C104740

The paper and board used in this book are made from wood from responsible sources

Orchard Books
An imprint of Hachette Children's Group
Part of The Watts Publishing Group Limited
Carmelite House, 50 Victoria Embankment, London EC4Y 0DZ

An Hachette UK Company
www.hachette.co.uk
www.hachettechildrens.co.uk

GLENDOR
THE STEALTHY SHADOW

BY ADAM BLADE

ORCHARD

> OCEANS OF NEMOS:
THE PRIMEVAL SEA

CLIFFS

ATHALAR

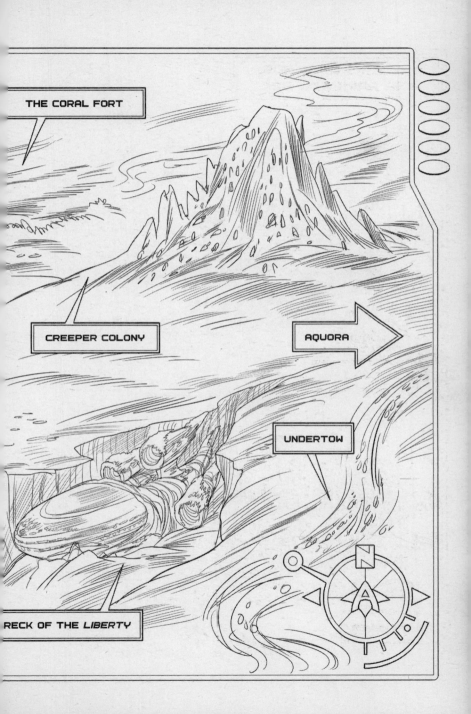

>TRANSMISSION FROM THE STARSHIP
LIBERTY

Any who threaten the SS *Liberty*
must die.

For 2,000 years I have lain at the
bottom of the ocean, forgotten.
For 2,000 years I have guarded my
ship. But my duty will never end:
analyse, react, destroy. Time may
have corroded my circuits, but I
have only grown more determined.

Now I have built four weapons to
aid me in my mission — creations
so powerful, nothing can stand
in their way. Enemies of the SS
Liberty beware. I will never stop
hunting you.

All threats must be terminated!

CHAPTER ONE
A CITY IN RUINS

The pale beams of Max's headlamps swam with silt as they pierced the gloom of the Primeval Sea, picking out crumbling pillars and domed buildings covered with straggly sea-moss.

Max's skin prickled as he scanned the decaying rubble – all that was left to mark where an underwater city had once stood. At the centre of the ruins, a colossal tower lay shattered. Max could just make out twisted hunks of dark red metal crushed beneath the fallen stones – the broken robotic body of Veloth the Vampire Squid. He looked for any flicker of movement, or the flash of a blinking light. There was nothing.

"Nasty squid, Max!" Rivet barked, his robotic voice blurting through Max's headset.

"Ex-squid now, Riv," Max said, turning towards his dogbot with a grin. Rivet was swimming alongside Max's sail sub, his metal tail wagging. On the other side of the dogbot, Max could see Lia, riding her swordfish, Spike. Lia was leaning low over Spike's back with her spear in one hand, frowning at the robotic remains below.

"That was no squid," she said firmly. "Squid are intelligent sea creatures. That was just a bunch of old metal and wires." Lia shot a glance at Rivet. "No offence, Rivet," she added.

Max shrugged. "Real squid or not, it almost

killed us. If Iris really does have three more Robobeasts, recovering the other elements is going to be tough."

Max glanced at the container on the dashboard before him. It had four compartments, each with a separate lid. Only one was full. It contained Flaric, the first of four alien elements needed to repair the damaged power core of Max's home city, Aquora. Max and Lia had harvested the Flaric from Veloth's battery pack. But they still had three more elements to collect – elements which had once powered the SS *Liberty*, an ancient spacecraft that had crashed into the Primeval Sea more than a thousand years ago.

Max swallowed, his mouth suddenly dry as he thought of how little time they had left – only a matter of days to find three elements, most likely implanted into robotic beasts created and controlled by Iris, the crazed AI computer system of the wrecked spaceship. If he failed, everyone in Aquora would die a slow and painful death of dehydration. Without power, the city had no way to purify more seawater. Once supplies ran out, the people were doomed.

Max drove his new sub, the *Silver Porpoise*, towards the edge of the ruined city, leaving the remains of Veloth behind. Lia rode Spike at his side, with Rivet just behind her. As they neared the outskirts, Lia pointed down through the murky water with her spear.

"Max, look!"

A cluster of statues stood at the edge of town, their swords and spears raised, like forgotten sentries guarding the borders. Lia's eyes were wide in the gloom. "They look almost like Merryn."

Max peered closer, and saw that she was

right. The statues had gills across their long necks, and webbed hands and feet, just like Lia. But instead of hair, they had thick fleshy tentacles. Most of the sculptures were missing arms or legs, and all of them were covered in barnacles and weed.

"The people who built those statues must have lived here once," Lia said, gazing sadly at the broken figures.

Max nodded. "Before Iris came along with her evil robots, and destroyed them all."

Iris. Max's chest tightened with dread at the memory of the computer's friendly, child-like holographic face. Intelligent Reactive Interference System. Whoever had programmed the artificial intelligence had meant for her to protect the spacecraft. But in the centuries since the SS *Liberty* had crashed, in the darkness below the ocean, Iris had gone haywire. She intended to wipe out all possible threats to her spaceship – which unfortunately meant every intelligent life form on Nemos.

Max clenched his teeth. *Not on my watch! Iris isn't getting anywhere near another city!* He glanced again at the ruins behind them. Once that place was filled with life, just like Sumara… A cold tingle shivered down his spine. He pushed his sub's thruster to full speed, suddenly eager to be away.

"So, where now?" Lia asked, accelerating at his side.

"Next element, Max?" Rivet barked, his propellers whirring to keep up.

Max glanced at the handheld energy tracker pad that his mother had given him, resting beside the Flaric container on his dashboard. It showed a map of the surrounding ocean. A blue light marked the sub's current location. Another, fainter, red light flickered near the top of the screen – the next of the elements that fuelled the SS *Liberty*.

Max led them onwards through the half-darkness of the silty water, heading for the coordinates of the blinking red light. A tingling on the back of his neck told him something was out there.

"Keep your eyes peeled," he told Lia. "There's something watching us. I can feel it." Each time he glanced into his rear viewer, or turned his head to the side, he caught a faint movement, as if something had just slipped out of view. He rubbed his eyes. *Maybe I'm imagining things…*

As they crested a rise in the ocean floor, the silvery light cast by the sub's headlamps glanced off a looming mass of rock ahead. Vast cliffs rose up from the seabed, almost blocking the way, with just a narrow, jagged gash showing a passage between them.

"I don't like the look of that," Max said, slowing the sub. The beams of the headlamps lit no more than a few sub-lengths ahead. In the gloom, Max thought he caught sight of a pale tentacle slipping into the shadows.

"Dark, Max!" Rivet barked, his eyes glowing like coals in the low light as he peered into the canyon.

"Let's see if we can find a way around these cliffs," Lia said. She slid from Spike's back and swam towards the opening. "It looks like we could get through here, but maybe we should go over— Spike! No!" Lia cried, as

Spike darted past her into the darkness. Lia put her hands to her temples, using her Aqua Powers to communicate with her swordfish.

After a moment she let her hands fall and turned back to Max, shaking her head. "He's not listening," she said. She bit her lip. "It's not like him at all. We'll have to go after him."

Max nodded. "Let's go!" He pushed the sail sub's throttle to full, and zoomed after Spike. The narrow gash opened into a flat valley with high rock faces overshadowing it on either side.

"Yuck!" Lia said, wrinkling her nose. The floor of the valley was hidden beneath a layer of black sludge, shimmering with oily greens and pinks in the light from Max's beams. Max could just make out the silvery shape of Spike in the distance, swimming backwards and forwards with his sword above the sludge, as if he were searching for something.

Lia groaned. "Whatever he's found, it had better be good!"

Max let his gaze run upwards, over the rocky walls that hemmed them in. His breath snagged in his throat. A line of slim silhouettes stood along the top of the underwater cliff. Tentacles flowed from their heads, like those of the statues in the town they had just left. But these tentacles snaked about in the water, and as Max watched, one figure lifted an arm, wielding a hefty looking blaster.

It's an ambush!

CHAPTER TWO
SERVANTS OF IRIS

Max angled his main beams up at the line of figures, his finger on the torpedo trigger. At least ten broad-shouldered creatures stared back at him coldly. A throaty roar rumbled through the ocean as three more of the creatures, riding bulky aquabikes, surged towards the cliff-edge. *They've got tech!* Max realised with shock. The unwieldy blasters and tarnished aquabikes looked roughly cobbled together.

Colourful paint streaked the creatures' green skin and spattered their rusted armour.

A tall figure with a narrow silver crown resting above his brows turned his gaze to Lia and held up his hand. "Do not be afraid," he called. "We shall save you and your swordfish from the evil servants of Iris!"

Max felt a stab of fear. "Where?" he cried, glancing about, expecting to see a Robobeast bearing down on him. He could see Spike, finally swimming back towards Lia, and Rivet, floating in the water nearby, but nothing else. But when he looked back up at the troops above, he noticed every weapon pointed at him. Realisation dawned on him slowly.

"Me?" Max said. "I'm not working for Iris!" But his words were swallowed by the throb of aquabike motors as the creatures swooped towards him.

"Lia! Let's go!" Max cried, flinging the *Silver Porpoise* into reverse.

"No!" the leader with the crown boomed, throwing up his hand. The creatures either side of him lifted their hands too, and their eyes began to glow an eerie electric green. The water swirled before them, blurring Max's view.

What's happening?

"Danger, Max!" Rivet barked. A huge, white, spinning column of water appeared before the creatures, and whirled towards Max's sub.

Whoa! They can control water!

Max steered sharply, but the column swerved too. His sail sub juddered as the whirlpool hit, spinning it around. The jolt of speed flipped Max's stomach, setting all his nerves jangling. His shoulder slammed into the wall of the craft. He tried to push away, but he couldn't. The force on his body was too strong. Through the watershield he caught glimpses of the canyon walls spinning around him.

"Get off me!" Lia snapped, her voice loud in his headset. "I don't need rescuing!"

Max squinted through the whooshing water and caught sight of her pulling her arm away from the creature with the crown. A moment later, she and Spike were surrounded by tentacled men and women riding aquabikes.

Max ignored the dizzy sickness building inside him and reached for his dashboard, flicking the switch to release the sub's metal spinnaker sail. There was a low hum and a clunk as the sail deployed like a parachute in front of the craft. The sub jerked, then leapt forwards out of the whirling current, leaving Max's stomach behind.

Max sat up, hit a button to retract the sail and shook his head to clear the dizziness. As soon as he could see straight, a huge, silver net filled his view with a dozen armoured creatures holding the edges. Max threw his sub into reverse, but before he could accelerate away, the net closed around the craft. Thick ropes of twisted metal pressed against the watershield.

"Trapped, Max!" Rivet barked from behind him. Max glanced into his rear viewer to see Rivet trussed up in another net, pulled behind the group of the Merryn-like creatures. Lia's arms were held tight by two sturdy women. The leader with the crown floated at her side, scowling fiercely at Max.

"Halt, friends of Iris!" the young man said, lifting his blaster, and aiming it through the windshield of Max's sub. Max considered using torpedoes. He could easily

blast through the net. But these creatures were enemies of Iris – innocent sea-folk. He couldn't risk hurting them – which meant he'd have to go along with them and sort things out the civilised way…

His chest burned with frustration at the thought. *We don't have time for this!*

Back in Aquora the water reserves were running out…

CHAPTER THREE
INSIDE THE CORAL FORT

"I'm not working for Iris," Max said, for what felt like the zillionth time. "Iris wants us dead, along with everyone else."

Max glanced to either side of him, taking in the slim, muscular forms of the creatures gripping his arms. The one on his right, a strong-looking figure with a slash of orange paint across his face, leered back at him and pointed a homemade blaster at Max's head.

"Okay, relax," said Max.

More tentacled creatures followed on ramshackle aquabikes, dragging Rivet and the *Silver Porpoise* in nets. Max could hear the laboured chug of the aquabikes' engines.

They really need some fine-tuning, he thought.

Ahead, he could see three female guards surrounding Lia. One held her confiscated spear, another Max's hyperblade. Spike swam free, but flitted anxiously beside them.

"Calm down," Lia said, soothingly. "We'll soon get this cleared up."

But Max was starting to doubt it would be that easy. He turned his attention to the tentacle-haired creature with the crown, riding his aquabike alongside them. Up close, the man looked younger than Max had imagined. His dark, deep-set eyes were overshadowed by a fierce frown, and he was chewing his lip as if worried.

He turned his frown on Max. "You say you are not working for Iris," he said, "but what proof do you have?"

"Don't listen to his lies, Prince Finn," the muscled guard cut in. "This boy could be the demon Iris's brother, they look so alike. They even use the same kind of tech. Just look at that dogbot with its glowing red eyes. Pure evil through and through."

Max let out an exasperated sigh and gestured to Lia and Spike ahead. "Look, if I were with Iris, what would they be doing with me? Lia's Merryn. All Merryn hate tech!"

Prince Finn shrugged. "You must have brainwashed the weak-minded ocean dweller," he said. "Which makes her just as dangerous as you are."

"Excuse me!" Lia's head snapped around. "I'm the daughter of the Merryn King Salinus – which makes me a princess, by the way – and

I've got more brains in my little finger than the lot of you seem to have all together! Dragging innocent strangers around at blaster-point? You should know better. What species are you, anyway?"

"We're the Sepha," the prince said. "I've never heard of the Merryn, or any king save my father. And since we're the ones holding the blasters, you might want to keep your opinions about our intelligence to yourself."

Lia looked back at Max, and rolled her eyes.

Max nodded. *We're not getting anywhere!*

The Sepha led them onwards over a seabed of steeply-rising rock. Spike swam close to Lia's side, and Rivet kept quiet inside his net, tugged behind the procession. The shallow water warmed around them until it felt almost like a bath. At the same time, it brightened from deep, murky blue to clear turquoise. Shafts of sunlight slanted from the sparkling surface above, outlining bulges and treelike-structures on the ocean floor ahead.

As Max and Lia were dragged closer, the shapes became clear, shifting to glowing pinks and reds. The whole seabed was covered with branching corals in every shade. Rainbow-coloured fish swam between the coral stacks, and spiny crabs and starfish crept over the living seabed. *It's beautiful,* Max couldn't help but think, despite his building frustration.

At the centre of the reef, a knobbly tower, as tall and broad as Max's apartment block in Aquora, rose through the water to break the glittering surface. The tower was a patchwork of corals in different colours and textures. Sepha with bandanas tied around their heads and paint on their cheeks aimed blasters from narrow windows. More patrolled the waters, wearing painted armour and carrying blasters, as well as swords and spears.

"It's a natural fortress!" Max said, gaping up at the tower. And now the Sepha's gaudy makeup didn't look odd at all. *It's camouflage!*

Ahead of him, Lia gasped. "But that's impossible!" she said. Max followed the line of her gaze right up to the top of the coral structure. Sepha were clambering from the water and into the open air above. "How can they leave the water without masks?" Lia said. "Can they breathe air?"

Prince Finn answered gruffly, "Since Iris made most of the ocean too dangerous for us to inhabit, we've been forced to adapt."

Lia stared back at the prince, her eyes wide with amazement. "But how?" she asked.

A proud smile flickered across the prince's stern face. He gestured to some fronds of dark kelp billowing up from the reef. "We harvest that kelp," he said. "When we eat it, a special bacteria from the weed becomes part of our body, living on our gills so we can breathe air. Without this discovery we would have been killed by Iris and her evil creations long ago."

Max and Lia exchanged an astonished glance. It didn't sound possible. But Max could *see* the Sepha leaving the water.

The prince led his convoy onwards towards a low, cave-like opening near the base of the fortress. Max and Lia were tugged inside, into a long low passageway lit by what looked like LED headlamps, screwed to brackets on the wall. Up close, the whole structure was crawling with crustaceans and bristling with anemones. The growl of aquabike engines echoed behind them as they followed the winding tunnel, deeper into the fortress.

Finally, Max was thrust into a huge, hollow atrium with twisting coral pillars reaching to a ceiling far above. The place buzzed with activity. Max could see at least twenty Sepha busy at driftwood benches, tinkering with bits of tech. Their tentacles were held back by bandanas, and goggles covered their eyes.

"A workshop!" Max said.

"Breather tech!" Lia said, wrinkling her nose. Piles of metal parts were pushed up against the walls, and more lay strewn on the floor. Max spotted turbines and engines stacked on top of each other, and a huge mound of metal legs and fins. Spike poked at the mound of body parts with his sword, dislodging a leg, then darted away with a click of alarm. A young Sepha woman unbent from her work on the rusting hulk of an aquabike and frowned as Max and Lia passed.

On the far wall of the cavern, a huge mural formed a backdrop to the busy workshop. Max recognised the abandoned city in which they had defeated Veloth painted on the pale coral, coloured in long strokes of blue and green. A crowd of Sepha were fleeing the city, hand-in-hand. Craned over them, her long fingers stretched out like talons, and her mouth spread into an evil grin, was the form of Iris, painted red.

He turned to Prince Finn and nodded at the mural. "Iris chased you from your city?"

The prince gestured to the blood-red figure.

"The demon Iris tried to destroy us," he said. "My ancestors had no choice but to flee from Athalar – our city – and take refuge here. But I will lead my people back to our true home. We will defeat Iris and her minions, whatever evil magic they wield."

"Iris isn't a demon," Max said. "She's a computer system gone wrong. She tried to kill us too back at your city, with a robotic squid. We defeated it by taking the Flaric from its battery pack. The powder was fuelling its weapons. It's not magic, it's just tech. We can help you defeat it."

The prince smiled bitterly and shook his head. "The demon Iris and her servants have fooled us before. We will not fall for her lies again." He turned to the guards surrounding Max and Lia. "Show the prisoners to their cells," he said. Then he pointed to Rivet, still bound tight in his metal net. "Dismantle that defence bot. We can copy its workings and create our own robotic creatures to fight Iris."

Max's stomach lurched as Rivet let out a frightened whimper.

"You can't!" he cried, but strong hands grabbed him under the arms and tugged him towards a dark, rounded hole in the wall, leaving Rivet and Spike behind. Max twisted and writhed in their grip, but there was nothing he could do. He felt like his heart might burst. *They're going to tear Rivet apart!*

CHAPTER FOUR

DOUBLE DOGBOT TROUBLE

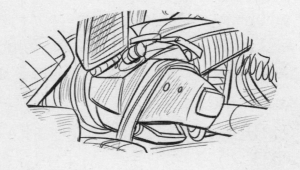

Rivet's confused barks echoed in Max's ears as he was bundled down a twisting tunnel.

"You can't take Rivet apart!" Max cried, turning to first one, then the other Sepha guard holding his arms. But both had their eyes fixed straight ahead.

"You have to listen!" Lia tried, fighting against two Sepha gripping her arms. "We've got nothing to do with Iris." But the guards held her tightly and were as silent as Max's.

The tunnel came to an abrupt end with a round doorway, leading to darkness. Max's arms were released. Before he could turn, a sharp shove between his shoulder blades forced him into a gloomy chamber. He spun to see Lia thrust into the cell after him. A door of twisting coral bars slammed shut across the entrance.

"Don't," Max cried. "You're making a big mistake!"

The guards locked the door with a click, then swam away.

Max swallowed hard and turned to Lia, his pulse thumping in his ears. "We have to get out of here and save Rivet. If they take him apart, all his memories and personality will be lost. He'll never be the same again!"

Lia frowned at the narrow coral bars that closed them in. "Getting out shouldn't be too tricky," she said, turning side-on to the door.

She lifted her leg and kicked.

Thud! Lia tumbled backwards into the cell, clutching her knee to her chest. "Ow!" The coral bars hadn't even shuddered.

"If only I had my hyperblade!" Max said. There was no way he could break those bars without it. He slumped to the floor, dark thoughts swirling through his mind. *Soon, Rivet's going to be junk metal, and Aquora's water supply will run out. I've failed…*

A soft, familiar clicking sound made his head snap up. A sleek shadow was darting down the tunnel towards them.

"Spike!" Lia cried, "I knew you'd come good!" Spike thrust his sword through the bars. Lia stroked her pet's head while Spike chattered gently. Lia chuckled.

"What did he say?" Max asked, leaping up.

"He's been trying to communicate with the Sepha," Lia said. "He thought he'd found more Merryn – that's why he led us towards them. But apparently they don't understand him at all. He says trying to talk to the Sepha is like trying to talk to plankton."

"Tell me about it!" Max said. "Spike? Can you get us out of here? Rivet needs us."

Spike rested the toothed edge of his sword against one of the coral bars and started to saw. It brought a sudden memory to Max's mind, of Rivet gnawing through the bars of their cell on their very first Sea Quest. An agonising pang squeezed his chest.

Please don't let us be too late!

Spike made short work of the bars, and soon a cut section fell free. Lia and Max squeezed out.

"Quickly, back to the main room. We don't have much time!" Max powered off, following Spike down the winding coral tunnels, swimming so fast his legs soon burned with the effort. But he couldn't let Rivet down.

When they reached the brightly lit workshop, Max gasped. *No!* The noise and flare of welding-torches filled the room. Rivet lay bound to a driftwood table with Prince Finn bent over his metal body, spanner and welding torch in hand. Beside him, two more Sepha were welding sheets of metal into an unmistakably dogbot-like shape.

Rivet's red eyes flashed with alarm. "Error!" he barked.

The prince glanced over his shoulder at Max, his welding torch hovering just above Rivet's belly. As his gaze met Max's, the Sepha's eyes narrowed. "How did you escape?"

"Don't hurt him!" Max cried. Spike swooped across the room towards the prince.

Finn spun and jabbed his sparking welding torch towards Spike, sending the swordfish

swerving away with a clack of terror.

"Hey!" shouted Lia. Get away from him!"
The prince tugged a sword from his belt,
made from scavenged metal. "Guards,
recapture the prisoners!" he shouted. A
dozen Sepha guards swarmed to their
leader's side, armed with a terrifying mix of

blasters, torches and drills.

"Er, any plan?" Lia muttered beside Max, gazing worriedly along the line of Sepha.

Max glanced frantically about the room. "We need our weapons…" He spotted his hyperblade along with Lia's spear buried in a pile of sheet metal and wires, lying in between them and the guards. "There they are. Go!" Max kicked his legs and sped towards the pile, with Lia on his tail. The Sepha warriors launched forward too, but Max and Lia got to the weapons first. Max snatched up his hyperblade, swinging it in arcs at the approaching Sepha. Lia jabbed her pearl spear, threateningly.

HWONK! HWONK! HWONK! The Sepha froze as the whole coral fort erupted in an ear-splitting alarm.

The prince was the first to move. "Iris is attacking," he cried, pointing his sword towards the exit to the coral fort. "Sepha! To your battle stations!"

Max's stomach clenched. *Just what we need!*

Around the large coral workshop, Sepha threw off their welding masks and zoomed towards the tunnel. Max tried to pick out a route to Rivet, but the way was still blocked by Finn and his personal guard.

"Stay with me," Finn shouted to the paint-streaked soldiers. "We'll take care of the prisoners." Finn and his guard shot towards Max and Lia, the prince lunging for Max with his sword, while the others rounded on Lia and Spike. "You did this!" Finn hissed, his blade flashing towards Max's head. "You brought Iris's minions here!"

Max parried the prince's blow with a powerful thrust, sending him reeling back, but three more Sepha were right behind their leader. Their swords glinted in the harsh light as they started to circle Max. *I can't fight them all.*

He glanced towards Lia and Spike, but both were busy, jabbing and thrusting at opponents of their own. *If only I had my sub,* Max thought, narrowly ducking a two-handed swipe from one of the prince's men.

Then he saw it. Resting against the back wall of the room was the *Silver Porpoise!* Max kicked upwards with all his strength, diving over the prince's head and the swiping swords of his troops.

"Stop him!" The prince shouted.

Max was already leaping inside the sub. He hit a red button on the dashboard. The plexiglass canopy slid over the cockpit and locked into place, the water draining away.

Clang! The prince's sword crashed down onto the hood and bounced off. Max fired the engine and aimed his blasters at the fuming prince and his men.

"Retreat!" the prince cried, diving out of the way as Max surged forwards. Max steered the sub towards Lia. She was fending off two tall Sepha with the butt of her spear.

"Lia, untie Rivet!" Max called. "I'll cover you!" He hit the accelerators and revved loudly towards Lia's opponents. Their eyes went wide with terror and they kicked away with their webbed feet.

Lia jumped onto Spike. "Get to Rivet!" They zoomed to where the dogbot was lying with his metal paws curled above his chest.

"Help, Lia!" the dog yelped.

"Keep still, Riv." Max felt a pang of relief as he saw Lia's spear come down with a snick, severing the ropes that bound Rivet to the table. The dogbot leapt up and threw himself at Lia, licking her face.

Lia pushed him away, smiling through a

grimace. "It's all right, Riv," she said. "You're safe. Now let's get out of here!"

"That way!" Max cried, pointing towards the tunnel that led from the fortress. Lia swam onto Spike's back, and she and Rivet powered into the winding cave. Max hit the turbos and followed in his sub, dodging Sepha swimming outside. He heard Finn's angry shouts, dying away in the sub's speakers.

Max gripped the steering lever, readying himself for what might await them outside the fort. What had Iris sent this time?

As soon as Max burst out into the glistening brightness of the coral reef, it was clear that the Sepha were in serious trouble. Terrified shouts and the clang of weapons echoed though the water. The whole reef was a chaos of swirling tentacles.

Two huge, mutated octopuses with luminous green spots were attacking the

paint-streaked figures, pulling them from their makeshift aquabikes. Shiny chips were embedded between the octopuses' eyes. *Iris's defence bots!* Last time Max and Lia had fought off mutated sharks enslaved by Iris with her robotic implants, but these octopuses looked just as dangerous. The creatures' powerful suckered limbs whipped about in a flurry, smashing blasters and swords from Sepha hands and lashing at their armoured bodies.

Max felt a wave of horror, as he saw one guard thrashing in the grip of a coil, while another was being forced towards a gaping beak. More Sepha were aiming spears at the robotic chips, trying to free the creatures from the control of Iris, but the defence bots' muscular limbs blocked them effortlessly.

"We've got to free them," Lia shouted, drawing back her spear and swooping towards the closest octopus, on Spike, leaving

Rivet paddling by the *Silver Porpoise*. Max took aim at the second colossal creature with his stun torpedoes. He had to be accurate. The torpedoes would only daze the octopus, but they were powerful enough to seriously harm the Sepha, and maybe even kill them.

"Destroy the demon's beasts!" cried a voice, behind Max. He looked back to see Finn darting from the coral tunnel, flanked by at least twenty Sepha guards. Lifting their blasters, they sent a hail of energy bolts towards the attacking octopuses.

"No!" Lia shouted. "Don't harm them! They're being controlled."

The octopuses can't dodge that, Max thought, as the volley of blaster bolts fell upon the enslaved creatures. Suddenly, both octopuses dropped their captives, and in the blink of an eye shrunk their massive rubbery bodies to the size of Rivet, drawing in their tentacles. The blaster bolts fizzed past them. One defence bot surged towards the seabed, its body expanding back to its normal size, taking cover behind a coral pillar, while trying to grab nearby Sepha. The other octopus made straight for Prince Finn, slaloming between energy bolts.

"Watch out!" Max spun his craft, aiming his torpedoes at the speeding octopus. The Sepha guards tried to shoot again, but the defence bot was already upon them, slapping them aside. Finn turned his own blaster on the writhing creature, but a long tentacle snapped out and knocked the gun from his hand. The defence bot's tentacle rippled around the prince's neck, coiling into a loop.

Finn let out a strangled yelp as the muscular tentacle flexed and squeezed, ready to crush the life from the Sepha prince.

CHAPTER FIVE

ALLIES

Max watched in horror through the water screen as the prince kicked and scrabbled in the defence bot's grip. "Out of the way," Max shouted to the prince's guards as they tried to get to their leader. "I'm going to fire my torpedoes."

"Don't shoot!" one of the guards cried.

"Hold your fire!" another screamed.

But the prince's face was turning blue, his eyes bulging.

I have to risk it! Max cranked the power

of his stun torpedoes down as far as they would go and hit fire.

Zap! The energy blast seared through the water and smacked the octopus in the side of the head. The creature jolted, its tentacles shooting straight out from its body.

Freed from the creature's grasp, the prince sank towards the seabed, clutching his throat. His personal guard rushed to his aid as the octopus shook itself, drew in its tentacles, then twirled in the water to face Max's sub. Its dark eyes flashed with fury.

Max stared back at the creature, fingers poised over the sub's controls.

The octopus's body bulged, then, with a powerful blast of water, it shot towards the sub, tentacles trailing behind it.

"Watch out, Max!" barked Rivet, trying to bite at the octopuses' streaming tentacles. But he was thrown aside.

ZAP! ZAP! Max sent two more stun blasts whizzing towards the speeding defence bot. They slammed into its body, making it judder to a halt. A young Sepha woman with purple lines painted around her eyes darted quickly towards the octopus and deftly tugged the silvery chip from the creature's head. The octopus's blank eyes flickered into focus. Then its enormous body domed and flexed, swimming away through the water, free from the control of Iris.

"Max – I could do with some help over here!" Lia's voice blurted through his headset.

Max turned to see Lia and Spike jabbing at the second octopus, alongside six Sepha warriors, all dodging the whirling tentacles.

Max revved his engines and zoomed towards the octopus, aiming his stun blaster at the creature's head. The blast hit the rubbery beast right between the eyes. It sagged like an empty glove, then began to sink downwards through the water. Lia quickly removed the control chip from the octopus, then put her hands to her temples. The freed sea animal opened its tentacles like a parachute, then shot away, vanishing into the blue.

"Bye bye!" barked Rivet, metal tail wagging.

Lia patted his head. "It says thank you for setting it free."

Max glanced around the reef to find the Sepha army watching them, silently.

The slim Sepha woman with the purple outlines to her eyes lifted a fist. "All hail the Breather!" she cried.

The rest of the Sepha turned towards their prince. He was still rubbing the red marks around his throat. He looked slowly from Max in his sub to Lia, then nodded. "Hail the Breather!" he cried. The Sepha all let out a cheer.

"I think you've got a fan club," Lia said. Max felt himself blushing.

When the shouts had finally died away, Prince Finn swam towards Max and Lia. "You saved my life," he said. "I am grateful to you. I apologise for imprisoning you. But Iris has taught us not to trust too easily."

Max scanned the stern, proud face of the young prince from behind his watershield. He could only imagine what it would be like spending a lifetime fighting Iris. He smiled. "No hard feelings," he said.

Lia held out her webbed hand. "Friends?" she said.

The prince grinned and shook it. "Friends!" he said.

"How long has Iris been attacking your people?" Max asked the prince.

The prince's smile vanished. "For centuries," he said. "Iris came to Athalar in the guise of a friend. She even taught us her language. But a few decades back, she turned against us, entrapping sea creatures with electronic chips, sending them to destroy our city. After my father went missing in battle, we created a fortress here. The kelp allows us to escape from her evil creations above the surface."

"How did you make your tech?" Max asked.

"We used Iris's own technology," Finn said. "Each time we defeated one of her robotic creations, we dismantled it and learned to create our own weapons. But each invention has cost us dearly. We owe you much for destroying her vampire squid. We had already lost too many Sepha to its evil." Max saw a spasm of pain cross the prince's face, but his mouth was set into a fierce, determined line.

"We will help you all we can," Max told the prince, "But the battle isn't over yet. Iris has three more Robobeasts out here somewhere, and—"

"Enemy approaching!" The cry came from a window high up on the coral fort.

Max spun, scanning the darker ocean beyond the reef, and saw a huge black shape forging slowly towards them. *So those defence bots were just the first wave!*

"Prepare to attack!" Prince Finn shouted. His troops moved like lightning, swooping together into formation – two dense clusters on either side of the reef.

The giant shape drew closer, its shadow a huge inky blot sliding over the bright colours of the reef below. Max's hand flickered to his torpedo button.

"Big fishbot, Max!" Rivet barked.

"Those octopuses were just a decoy to lead us into the open," Lia said, shifting her grip on her spear. Max nodded, looking round at the Sepha exposed in the water. There was no time to regroup.

With a sudden dart, the colossal Robobeast bore down on them. It was the size of a celerium tanker, and its metal hull was the same rusted metallic brown. Two enormous fan-shaped fins protruded from its sides, each edged with tooth-like spikes, the size of hyperblades. Its eyes were massive and blank – dark, lifeless windows.

"Wait till it's in range," Finn shouted.

As the vast creature drew to a halt before them, the Robobeast's mouth gaped open. Max could see powerful hydraulic hinges on each side of its head, acting as jaws. Curved blades jutted from its metal gums like teeth.

"Prepare to open fire!" Prince Finn cried. But Max's stomach sank as he glanced at the Sepha formations. Many were already hurt, their armour battered, and their primitive

aquabikes were spluttering badly. Max guessed their outdated blasters wouldn't even dent the creature's thick metal hull.

Max took a deep breath, turning back to the Robobeast, adrenaline coursing through his veins as he waited for the Robobeast to attack. *No turning back now.*

CHAPTER SIX
SECRET WEAPON

Max scanned the robot's metal hull, looking for its weapons. All he could see was a silver box on the side of its broad head. The battery pack.

"Turn back, slave of the demon Iris," called Prince Finn. But his voice wavered with fear.

The robot's massive eyes blinked into life, casting long beams of light through the water. Max squinted into the brightness to see a holographic image – a young girl with a snub nose and cropped, dark hair.

"It's Iris," said Lia, disgust in her voice.

Max clenched his jaw. The large holographic face was smiling, showing two rows of perfectly straight teeth. But her eyes shone with a cold, hard light – clever, calculating and chillingly insane.

Iris lifted her hand and pointed a finger at Max. "I've been watching you," she said. "You thought Veloth was quite dead, didn't you? But its camera was still working, and

I saw you sneak away. I had two of my little defenders follow you here and you didn't even notice!" Iris tutted and shook her head, making her hair swing. "I'll find you, wherever you go. Soon enough, you'll tell me everything I need to know to protect my ship."

"You'll get nothing from us," Max shouted.

Iris's smile tightened and her green eyes flashed red. "You will tell me the coordinates of Aquora and Sumara," she said. "Glendor, my Robobeast, will make sure of that. And once I've finished with the Sepha, I'll go and annihilate both cities." With that, her image flickered and vanished, leaving Max blinking into the darkness of Glendor's hollow eyes. The colossal robot still didn't move, except for the faint sculling motion of its fins.

"What's it doing?" Lia asked. "Why isn't it attacking?"

"I can't see any guns," Prince Finn said, peering at the monster.

"It will have some sort of weapon," Max said, "probably powered by an element in its battery pack."

"Well, let's not wait to find out what!" Finn said. "Troops! Take aim!" he shouted.

The Sepha guards all moved at once in their tight formations, placing the butts of blasters to their shoulders and aiming at Glendor's metal hull.

The reef lit up red as the Sepha opened fire, peppering Glendor with sizzling energy bolts. From his position behind their ranks, Max brought his fist down on his own torpedoes, adding his fire power into the mix.

He felt a chill of dread as he saw all the energy bolts bounce off Glendor without leaving a mark. Then slowly, steadily, the bloated robot started to creep forwards.

"Hold your ground!" the prince cried. The Sepha kept firing, trailing the moving Robobeast with their blasters, shooting round after round, even as the gigantic form of Glendor sailed overhead, plunging them into darkness. Glendor's wings lit up an eerie electric blue. Max suddenly felt sick. The Sepha were right beneath the beast.

"Call them back!" he told the prince. But at the same moment streams of crackling energy shot from the underside of the wings, striking the Sepha like lightning bolts. The men and women let out strangled cries of alarm as the weapons flew from their hands and whizzed towards Glendor's fins, surrounded by the sparking blue light.

One heavily armoured guard tumbled over in the water, arms and legs flailing as he was dragged upwards towards Glendor, a halo of

energy engulfing his metal armour. *Thunk!*
The man hit Glendor's wing, breastplate first,
and stuck fast. Everywhere, Sepha began to
be pulled towards the huge Robobeast by the
glowing energy beams.

Clank! Clunk! BANG! The Sepha stuck to
the Robobeast's magnetic wings, like flies
to a trap. Soon nearly all the warriors were
attached.

"People stuck on fishbot!" Rivet barked, hovering by Max.

"What evil magic is this?" the prince growled.

"Not magic," Max said, trying to swallow his rising horror. "Magnetese. One of the elements from SS *Liberty's* engine core. It's powerfully magnetic."

"I don't understand," the prince said.

"It means that giant fish can suck up anything made of metal," Lia said. "You need to get your armour off, quick! And Max, you need to get that sail sub out of here!"

Glendor's fins gave a powerful flick, and it surged forwards. A chorus of terrified cries erupted from the Sepha beneath it. The vast fins lit up, crackling all over with electric blue light. Prince Finn started to squirm out of his breast plate, but a before he could get it off, a sizzling bolt hit his chest and snatched him up like a lasso.

Max hit the sail sub's thrusters and steered sharp left just as a shimmering blue beam of energy knifed towards his sub.

"Rivet! Swim!" he shouted into his headset. But a moment later he heard a terrified yelp. He glanced into his rear viewer to see Rivet shooting upwards, dragged by a magnetic beam. Rivet hit the underside of Glendor's wing and stuck fast next to the struggling prince.

"Fish caught Rivet, Max!" Rivet barked.

In his rear viewer Max saw another glowing beam heading for his sub. He banked sharply, swerving towards the seabed, and the beam fizzed by, millimetres from the *Silver Porpoise*. Glendor plunged after him, its huge frame skimming the coral reef. *I've got to shake it,* thought Max. He swerved through the bright red branches of coral trees and between huge yellow boulders, shaped like brains.

Against the rushing water, Max could hear the yells of the Sepha alongside his dogbot crying out in panic as Glendor surged after his sub.

A sudden swift movement in his rear-viewer caught his eye, and he looked back to see Lia on Spike's back, streaking towards Glendor from behind, her spear raised to strike.

"What are you doing?" Max shouted to her.

"Distracting it!" Lia replied, smashing the sharp point of her spear into the robotic fish's back. She pulled her weapon free and sliced it down again, but as it struck, Glendor's huge wing swept upwards, slamming into Spike and knocking Lia spinning from the swordfish's back. Glendor's blunt snout snapped around. Its dark eyes fixed on Lia's tumbling body, then it shot through the water, mouth gaping wide as a cave-opening.

"Hold on, Lia!" Max heaved at his wheel, spinning his sub around after the giant robot. He engaged his torpedoes, ready to fire, but he couldn't risk it – not with Rivet and all the Sepha hanging helplessly from Glendor's fins. *I need to dislodge that battery pack!* Max realised.

He engaged his turbos, the seascape below him melting in a blur of speed. Ahead, he could see Lia righting herself, looking about for Spike. When she saw Glendor powering towards her, her eyes went wide with panic. She kicked her legs, knifing through the water like only a Merryn princess could.

"Go, Lia!" Max yelled, but the huge winged fish rocketed after her.

Max pushed the sail sub as fast as it would go, drawing closer to the Robobeast. He kept his eyes fixed on the tiny box of the battery pack. *I need something to lever it off.* Then he realised. *The sail!* He flipped a switch and felt his sub judder as his side sail unfurled. Lia's slender form streaked along ahead of the Robobeast, looking back at what Max was doing.

"Quickly," she called to him, just dodging clear of the creature's snapping jaws.

I have to get this right! Max held the craft straight, travelling at exactly the same speed as Glendor, his eyes on the silver box… Gently, he angled the craft, leaning the tip of the sail towards the battery pack. *Almost got it…*

The Robobeast slowed suddenly. *SCREECH!* The tip of the sail hit Glendor's side hard, scraping along the dull metal. The impact jolted through Max's body as his sub lurched violently, rolling round and round.

Max tugged at the wheel, white water swirling across the viewing screen. He reached for his dashboard and managed to hit a switch to furl his sail, wrestling the sub steady.

"Max, look out!" Lia shouted through his headset.

Max glanced into the rear viewer, and terror jolted through his body. Glendor's vice-like metal mouth was opening behind

him. And that wasn't the worst part. Blue magnetic energy flickered around Glendor's teeth, and the next moment, a bright bolt streamed out straight towards Max's sub.

Max's heart thumped as he slammed the thrusters to full, but he knew it wouldn't be enough. The cockpit lit up, electric blue, and Max was thrown forward on his seat, face smashing against the dashboard, tears blurring his vision. *It's got the sub!* The engines screamed and stuttered, fighting the magnetic force. But it was no use. The sub began to slip backwards, into Glendor's jaws. There was no escape. Through the watershield Max could see the tips of glinting, knife-like teeth closing around him.

CHAPTER SEVEN
WEAPON STORM

Max hit the release for the *Porpoise's* hood. *Whoosh!* Cool water flooded the cabin, buoying him up. He kicked hard against his seat, catapulting himself out of the vessel, just as the Robobeast's glowing blue teeth sank into the metal hull of the sail sub.

"Max! Over here!" Lia cried. She and Spike were floating near the ocean bed behind a huge cactus-like pillar of coral. Max dived to her side, panting hard, then peered out to see Glendor's vast, bloated form turn and swoop back overhead. The great robotic creature spat out the dented sail sub like a morsel of food, then zapped it with its magnetic beam, pulling the vessel against its wide fins where it missed a terrified Sepha woman by a hand's breadth.

Kicking, screaming Sepha covered the underside of the Robobeast, all crying out in panic. "Help us!"

"I can't move."

"Get us off here!"

Max caught a glimpse of Rivet's flashing eyes among the struggling men and women. He turned to Lia. "We have to help them!"

"How? That thing is too powerful!" Lia said.

Max watched Glendor circling above them, the size of an Aquoran battleship. *What has it got planned next?*

A low, humming vibration shuddered through the water, coming from the

Robobeast's wings. It reminded Max of Rivet's electromagnet, and he suddenly had a very bad feeling. Patches of Glendor's wings flickered from blue to deep, dark red, and the metal attached to those areas rattled and shook. Max's heart hammered with horror.

"We won't need to get them down," he said. "Glendor's reversed the magnets. Its wings are turning to repel!"

A blaster stuck to a red part of the Robobeast's fin suddenly span away, whizzing straight towards Max's head. He dodged behind the pillar, the metal object whining past his ear. Max ducked and Lia pulled Spike down as another larger projectile, glowing red, fired past them.

"Stay down!" Max shouted. Spike let out a clack of alarm and Max and Lia huddled closer to the pillar. The large coral cactus began to shudder as a hail of metal objects smashed into it, others shooting by, sending up clouds of choking grit from the seabed. The deafening chorus of metal smashing into coral filled the reef.

Max poked his head out from behind the pillar, trying to catch sight of Glendor. But a large aquabike was heading in their direction. With a sudden tug, he felt his metal headset fly from his head, tumbling away through the water in a flash of red.

"Oh!" Lia grabbed for her own headset, but it shot away after Max's.

BOOM! The pillar protecting them exploded from the impact of the aquabike smashing into it. Rubble pattered against Max's body and filled his gills and eyes. He felt a jolt of fear. They were in the open now! Glendor had turned its entire wings to repel, and a tide of shimmering metal blasters and sharp weapons whizzed towards them, followed by the heavier Sepha, building up speed as they flailed in halos of red light.

"Swim for it!" Max told Lia.

Lia dived onto Spike's back and, with a flick of his tail, they were gone, dodging between projectiles. Max followed as best as he could through the deadly storm, kicking his legs and wheeling his arms to dodge hurtling objects.

Max saw that many of the paint-streaked Sepha were on course to hit the coral fort. Weapons and hunks of broken aquabike slammed into the walls ahead of them, smashing off bright lumps of living rock. Max grabbed at a Sepha woman as she rocketed past him, but her arm was snatched from his grip.

"We need to stop them somehow," Lia cried. But Max didn't see how they could. He could hardly bear to watch.

"Use your magic!" Max caught sight of the prince streaming through the water, his eyes glowing bright as he shouted to his people. "Use the power of water to save yourselves!"

The prince held up his hand, closing his eyes, as the water before him started to swirl in a fierce current. The churning whirlpool dragged him away over the fort at the last second. Behind him, the Sepha tumbling towards the fortress held up their hands too, conjuring a huge swirling current to pick them up, carrying them past the coral fortress. Max felt his own body jerk him sideways, as he too was caught up in a giant whirlpool, swirling round and round, side by side with the Sepha. It was like a graceful underwater dance.

"Their Aqua Powers are counteracting Glendor's magnetic force!" shouted Lia, a grin on her face as she too spun round, in between Sepha.

The red glow shed by Glendor's wings faded, then went out. "It must be recharging," Max yelled. He heaved an exhausted sigh of relief.

The Sepha lowered their hands, and the spinning current gradually slowed. Blasters, swords and aquabikes drifted slowly towards the seabed. Max saw his sail sub settle gently onto the coral beside Rivet. The dogbot shook himself, then paddled towards Max. "Dizzy!" he barked.

Max rubbed the dog's metal belly. "I'm glad you're safe, boy."

Sepha warriors swarmed towards their leader. In the gloom cast by Glendor's fins Max saw one man bleeding badly from a cut on his arm. Another had a torn tentacle. But they were all alive.

"Quick! Tell your people to take off their armour," Max called to Prince Finn.

The prince nodded. "Remove all metal!" he commanded his troops. "Iris's minion will not be able to capture you then!"

The Sepha quickly shed their helmets and breastplates, letting them fall to the coral seabed. Glendor hung above them, dark and ominously still.

"Get out of the water!" Max cried.

"Do as he says, quickly!" Prince Finn shouted. "Onto the fort!"

The Sepha kicked up through the water, their outlines blurring as they clambered above the surface, heaving themselves on top of the coral fortress.

"Lia! We have to get to the surface, too," Max said. "Put on your Amphibio mask!"

Lia glanced worriedly at Spike. "Go and hide," she told her swordfish. Spike nuzzled up to her for a moment, then with a reluctant click of agreement, flicked his tail and sped away. Lia put her hand to her throat, where her Amphibio mask usually hung, and the colour drained from her cheeks. "Glendor's magnetic beams ripped my mask off!" she said. "I can't breathe out of the water!" Cold horror washed over Max.

A hideous metallic clatter started up from Glendor's wings, as it began to glow blue, and once again metal objects began to fly through the water towards it, including the Sepha's discarded armour. Max and Lia froze. Once it had gathered more missiles, it would turn its magnets to repel again...

Max put his hand on Lia's shoulder. "I'm not leaving you here in the water with that thing."

There was a splash from above, and suddenly Prince Finn was swimming towards them, holding out a billowing frond of kelp.

"Here," he said, pushing the kelp into Lia's hand. "Eat it, quickly."

Lia took a hurried bite and swallowed. Her eyes met Max's for a moment, full of fear.

Glendor's massive wings turned red.

"Come on!" Max said. Lia nodded, then kicked her legs and swam for the surface beside Prince Finn. Max followed as fast as he could, finally breaking the surface. He saw an expanse of craggy coral, sticking out from the water, crowded with Sepha. He scrambled out of the water, feeling the sharp, brittle coral bite his palms. Lia stood, blinking in the sunlight, her fingers gently brushing her gills. Max held his breath. And then Lia smiled.

"I'm breathing!" she said. "I'm breathing air. It's so…so… I can't describe it!"

"It is amazing," Prince Finn said, grinning. "And what's more, Glendor can't get us up here!"

Max couldn't help smiling too to see his friend above the surface without a mask.

Now she's a Breather, just like me!

But there was no time to celebrate. He cast a glance down through the glittering water. He couldn't make out the details, but he could see the broad expanse of Glendor's glowing wings. As he watched, the wings started to change shape. It looked as if they were getting narrower. *No!* Max felt a jolt of fear. The wings weren't changing shape. They were tilting – turning upwards so they faced towards the sky!

"Look out!" Max yelled. An arsenal of shadowy shapes, outlined with shimmering red, hurtled towards the surface, then burst into the air in an explosion of water and spray. Aquabikes, blasters and breastplates arched high into the sky, surrounded by sparkling droplets.

Max looked round desperately at the crowd of Sepha, cowering on the rocky platform.

There was nowhere to hide.

Above, the metal objects blocked out the sun. Then they began to fall...

CHAPTER EIGHT

IRIS TAKES CONTROL

"Quick, to the other side!" Max turned and ran alongside Lia and the fleeing Sepha guards, towards the other end of the fortress. "Woah!" Max leapt back as a sword slammed into the coral fort point-first and sank right up to the hilt.

Cries of terror filled the air, along with the crunch of splintering coral, as aquabikes, blasters and armour hammered down around them. Max saw a Sepha man take a glancing blow to his scalp and stumble. "Get up!" Max shouldered the man to his feet, then helped him run on.

A huge shadow began to grow around Max, and he felt an icy wave of dread. He glanced up. The shining underbelly of the *Silver Porpoise* was plummeting towards his head! He couldn't get out of the way. Time

seemed to slow. *This is it,* he thought.

Thud! Something cannoned into Max's side, knocking the air from his lungs and sending him sprawling, just as the sub slammed into the spot where he had been standing. Beside Max, Rivet watched him, eyes glowing bright.

"Rivet save Max!" he barked, wagging his tail.

"Thanks, Riv," Max said. He noticed with relief that the crash of falling weaponry had fallen silent. He scanned the coral to see the Sepha huddled in groups. Lia and Finn picked their way gingerly towards him through a field of swords and blasters sticking out of the ground like ugly plants.

"It looks like Glendor's run out of missiles," Lia said.

"Which means this is our chance," Finn said. "We need to work out how to defeat that thing. We can't stay up here forever, my people will starve."

"And we need that Magnetese!" Max said.

"Someone's going to have to go down there and face that Robobeast," Lia said.

Max squared his shoulders. "Now there's no more metal down there, Glendor can be defeated." He turned to the prince. "You should stay here to protect your people. I'll go."

The prince pulled out a long, thin sword, that had been embedded in the coral. "Then take my blade," he said, handing the sword to Max. "And good luck."

"I'm coming too," Lia said, holding up her coral spear. "After all, Spike's still down there."

"And me!" Rivet barked.

Max nodded to Lia but shook his head at the dogbot. "You can't, Riv. You're made of metal. Glendor will use you as a cannonball. Lia and I will go. We need to get that battery pack off."

Rivet whined. "Come back, Max."

Max scratched Rivet's ears. He swallowed his growing fear, then paced towards the edge of the island of coral. "We'll need to keep close underwater," he said to Lia. "Without our headsets, we won't be able to communicate otherwise."

Lia nodded grimly. "Let's go." She lifted her arms and dived into the water without a splash. Max leapt in behind her.

Beneath the waves, nothing stirred. Max could see the damage that had been done to the reef, lashed with dark pock-marks and jagged gashes. There wasn't a fish in sight. A hot wave of fury burned through Max's veins. *Iris won't rest until she's destroyed everything!*

Glendor hovered in the distance – a monstrous shape casting a dark blot over the broken reef. Its dead, hollow eyes seemed to be watching Max. Still, it didn't move.

"What is it waiting for?" Lia asked. Then she gasped. "What's that?"

A tiny silver bullet whizzed towards them through the water. Max grabbed Lia's shoulder and tugged her out of the way, but the bullet stopped dead. "It's some kind of capsule," said Max. The silver metal sparked, and started to glow as red as blood.

"This doesn't look good," said Lia, hefting her spear.

Scarlet filaments of liquid metal spread from the capsule and swirled around it, like tendrils of a jellyfish. The rippling filaments began to grow in size and glow brightly, like a computer screen, interlacing to create a flickering object. The rippling metal form began to shape itself into a figure, features forming on a glaring red face: a slim, smiling girl dressed in a jump suit.

"Iris," said Max. The metal capsule formed a bright buckle to Iris's belt.

"How's she doing that?" Lia asked.

Max scanned the form of the crazy computer. "Metal plasma," he said. "It has to be. Held together by a magnet in that capsule."

"Very clever!" Iris said, her voice crackling with static. "Now, down to business. I need those coordinates." Her lips twisted into a horrible smile. "The death of your friend should convince you that I'm serious." Her head snapped around and she stared at

Lia. Two bright lasers shot from her eyes, stabbing towards Lia's chest.

No! Horror threw Max towards his friend faster than he could think. He pushed Lia out the way, the lasers just burning his sleeve.

Beneath, Max saw a swirl of sleek silver fins. *Spike!* Max and Lia grabbed hold of

the swordfish, swinging onto Spike's back and zipping away.

Max glanced back to see the glowing plasmagram of Iris narrow her eyes in fury. She flew through the water up towards Glendor, settling astride the monstrous Robobeast. The giant metal creature flicked its colossal fins and surged forwards, far faster than Max had seen it move before.

"Tell Spike to keep low!" Max told Lia. "Use the coral as cover!"

Spike sped onwards, slaloming between red and pink coral trees and knobbly pillars, but the combined weight of Max and Lia was slowing him down. Glendor easily kept pace above them. Max glanced up to see Iris glaring at him, her eyes glinting with a deadly red light.

"You can't escape me!" she snarled. "All threats must be terminated." Forked red lasers shot from her mad, staring eyes.

CRACK! A tower of coral exploded into dust beside them, clogging Max's gills. *SMACK!* Another sizzling beam hit the seabed ahead, leaving a gaping hole. Max blinked away the grit and glanced over his shoulder. *Whoa!* More bright red lasers were streaking towards them. One zapped by so close Max could feel the heat frazzling the hairs on his arms.

"We can't keep dodging these lasers," Lia said. Max knew she was right.

Suddenly, a strong current grabbed hold of the swordfish and his riders, snatching the breath from Max's gills and spinning them round. He clung to Spike with his knees, blinded by the whirling current, Lia's arms squeezing him tight. Max knew what the currents meant… Sepha!

As quickly as it had whipped up, the current died, leaving them at the foot of the coral fort. Sepha were climbing down into the water, while others, already beneath the waves, let their hands fall to their sides.

"They saved us with their Aqua Powers!" Lia said. A metal object plunged into the water beside the tentacle-headed warriors, trailing bubbles. It was Rivet, wagging his tail hopefully as he powered towards Max.

"Rivet! No!" Max shouted. "Get out of the water before Glendor sucks you up!"

Rivet's ears drooped and his tail fell, but he turned and swam off. And as Max watched his dogbot go, an idea struck him – a Rivet-shaped idea. He slid from Spike's back.

"Lia! Can you and Spike keep Iris busy for just a little bit longer? I think I know how to use Glendor's magnetic force to defeat it once and for all."

"How?" Lia asked.

Max grinned. "I'm going to give it a bad case of indigestion!"

CHAPTER NINE

EXPLOSIVE INDIGESTION

Max swam as fast as he could along the tunnel that led into the Sepha fortress, the sizzle of Iris's energy blasts echoing around him. *Lia and the Sepha won't be able to keep Iris busy for long. I have to be quick!* He burst into the Sepha workshop and hurriedly looked around. *There!* The replica Rivet lay on the table where he'd last seen it. A spark of hope stirred in his chest, but he needed more tech for his plan to work – and a lot of luck.

Max swam to the rusted aquabike he'd noticed before. He flipped open the engine compartment. Inside, he found the most outdated, corroded, unstable-looking fuel cell he'd ever seen. *I'm surprised this thing didn't blow up as soon as it turned a corner. It's perfect!* The container oozed thick, yellow celerium fuel, but was still mostly full. And there were a pair of old-fashioned spark-plugs inside the engine too. Max snatched up a screwdriver. The screws were rusted, but with a few well-aimed blows, it didn't take long to get the engine out.

He hefted the oozing engine over to the bench where the replica Rivet lay. Its belly compartment hung open, ready for its new cargo. Max gently lifted the corroded engine inside. Thuds and cracks shuddered through the chamber around him, making the table

shake. *I hope they're okay out there!* But Max knew he couldn't head out yet. For his plan to work, his dogbot would have to be convincing.

He scanned the tables and piles of tech, looking for the final piece. *Yes!* He spotted two chips with red LED bulbs – probably the eyes from an old robot created by Iris – just right for the dogbot's eyes.

Max grabbed two batteries, wire-cutters and a reel of wire, then got to work wiring them up to the lights. He felt a tug of relief as the LEDs glared brightly. Next, Max screwed the blinking lights into the replica Rivet's eye sockets.

He stood back, and ran his eyes over the dogbot on the bench. It wasn't pretty. *But it will have to do!* He took a deep breath, gripped his screwdriver, then carefully drove it through the rusted metal of the aquabike's fuel cell. Immediately, a thin stream of highly explosive celerium drifted out. Max carefully closed the metal door that covered the replica Rivet's belly. Then he gently picked up the dog-shaped hulk, keeping it level, and headed for the door.

The tunnel shook and fragments of coral rained from the ceiling as Max swam, cradling his fragile creation in his arms, shielding it from the debris. Max prayed that the fuel cell wouldn't explode.

As he neared the fortress entrance, he carefully shifted his grip on the dogbot, holding it at arm's-length. He needed it to look as if the dogbot was pulling him along. Max kicked his legs out behind him. *Please don't blow up on me!*

Max swam from the entrance of the fortress, and at once he saw the giant Robobeast hovering over the reef. Iris's plasmagram sat on its back, grinning fiercely. The Sepha army swarmed around the Robobeast, jabbing it with coral spears and dodging the smouldering energy blasts shooting from Iris's eyes. "All of you will be destroyed," the plasmagram yelled.

Max swam up towards the Robobeast, arms straining to keep the Rivet bomb as stable as possible. He spotted Spike diving towards one of Glendor's massive wings. From Spike's back, Lia slashed out with her spear, denting the metal. Beside her, the prince stabbed out with a coral sword.

"Lia! Finn!" Max shouted. "Get everyone away from Glendor."

Lia eyed the dogbot in Max's hands and smiled. "Trust him," she said to Finn.

The prince nodded. "Retreat!" he yelled. The Sepha turned and dived as one, moving with the speed and grace of a shoal of fish. Prince Finn and Lia swooped after them.

Now it's up to me. Max swam out in front of Glendor's open jaws, holding his dog-bomb before him. The robot's glassy eyes turned until Max could see his own reflection in their depths, the red LED eyes of the dogbot in his hands blinking steadily back at him.

A blue glow flickered around the robotic fish's teeth. Then a lasso of magnetic energy snapped out towards the dog-bomb, snatching it from Max's hands. The beam pulled the bomb speeding towards the robot's widening jaws. Max turned his gaze upwards towards Iris. Her crazed grin broadened as her eyes locked with his. Max smiled smugly back at her.

Iris glanced at the dogbot rushing through the water, and for a moment, she looked confused, before her eyes shot wide open with horror.

"Glendor! No!" She shouted. But it was too late. Glendor's huge mouth snapped shut over the replica dogbot. Max felt a swell of triumph, then braced himself…

BOOM!

A blue-white cloud of foaming water exploded outwards from Glendor's head, snatching Max up and sending him tumbling head-over-heels towards the fort. When Max hit the coral wall he clung on, pressing his body against it.

Boof! A tremendous shockwave buffeted his body, tugging at his hair and clothes, threatening to suck him back out towards Glendor.

Then all was silent and still.

Max peered into the clearing water to see Glendor drifting down to the reef, its metal jaws hanging open. A huge, gaping hole had been blasted from its hull. Iris's plasmagram shimmered on its back, but Max saw immediately that there was something wrong with it. One side of Iris's liquid metal face was smeared downwards like squashed clay. Her whole body was flickering. Her misshapen mouth tried to shout but no sound came out. Her capsule must have been damaged in the blast! The top of Iris's head suddenly stretched out into the water like an elastic

band and her whole body twisted, pulling in different directions.

Then suddenly, the damaged plasma was sucked entirely back inside the tiny silver capsule. It hung in the water for a moment, then whizzed away through the water.

A huge cheer went up from the Sepha gathered at the base of the fort.

"That wasn't pretty!" Lia said, arriving at Max's side on Spike, with the prince swimming close behind. "Do you think we've seen the last of her?"

"Unlikely," Prince Finn said, smiling grimly. "She'll be back. She always comes back."

"At least you've got plenty of metal to make new aquabikes and weapons to fight her with," Max said, gesturing towards the battered remains of Glendor. "And we're not leaving the Primeval Sea until Iris is defeated once and for all. Which reminds me," Max turned to Lia. "We have some Magnetese to collect."

Max swam up to the top of the coral fort, and clambered out of the water. The *Silver Porpoise* sat amongst the metal debris. It was badly dented, tooth marks all over it. But Max could see the damage was only to the hull, and the engines would be fine.

Nearby on the coral, Max saw the container his mother had given him. He breathed a sigh of relief when he found the Flaric powder still safe inside. He scanned the rest of the wreckage, collecting together his energy tracker and communications gear. Lia's headset looked a little dented, but nothing Max couldn't fix.

He dived back into the water, taking the element container with him.

When Max reached Glendor's sunken form, Lia was already there on Spike, prising the battery pack from the side of the Robobeast's head with the tip of her spear.

"Careful!" Max said.

Lia shot him a look. "I AM being careful!" she said. At last the battery pack came free and Lia reached inside, pulling out a lump of putty-like metal. Max opened his container and Lia dropped the soft, highly magnetic element inside.

"Two down and two to go!" Max said. Lia grinned.

There was a tremendous splash from above, and Max looked up to see Rivet powering down through the water, pushing the lightweight sail sub with his snout.

"Rivet to the rescue!" Rivet barked.

Max smiled. "Thanks, Riv!" he said. He swam into the sub, and Rivet got in beside him. The energy tracker on the dashboard showed a blinking red light to the north. The next element had to be close.

Suddenly Max felt his energy sag. He couldn't help thinking of all the time they'd lost fighting Iris. By now, water in Aquora had to be running dangerously low. A wave of anxiety swelled in his chest. *What if we're too late?*

He shut the hood of his sub, and looked back towards the coral fort.

Prince Finn waited outside, surrounded by his personal guards. As Max watched,

Finn lifted his hand, and waved. The sight gave Max an idea. He turned on his sail sub's speakers.

"Goodbye, Prince Finn," he called. "Hey, a little boost would be nice!"

The prince smiled and held his hands, palms out, before him. His eyes glowed bright, and a white surge of water rushed over the reef towards Max's sub.

"Big wave, Max!" Rivet barked.

Max hit the switch to deploy his sails and angled his sub to catch the powerful current. Beside him Spike lifted his sword and Lia held tight to her swordfish's back.

WHOOSH! The surge of water hit the sub, and, with the sudden rush of speed, Max felt his spirits lift as they shot away from the coral fortress. *We've destroyed two of Iris's creations already. If anyone can defeat her and save Aquora, it's us!*

Don't miss Max's next Sea Quest adventure,

when he faces

MIRROC
THE GOBLIN SHARK

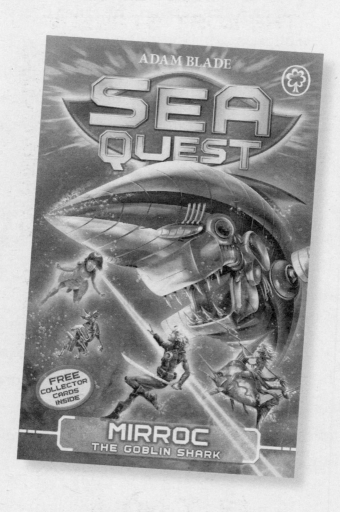

COLLECT ALL THE BOOKS
IN SEA QUEST SERIES 7:
THE LOST STARSHIP

FREE COLLECTOR CARDS INSIDE!

VELOTH
THE VAMPIRE SQUID

978 1 40834 064 6

GLENDOR
THE STEALTHY SHADOW

978 1 40834 066 0

MIRROC
THE GOBLIN SHARK

978 1 40834 068 4

BLISTRA
THE SEA DRAGON

978 1 40834 070 7

OUT NOW!

Look out for all the books in
Sea Quest Series 8:

THE LORD OF ILLUSION

GORT THE DEADLY SNATCHER
FANGOR THE CRUNCHING GIANT
SHELKA THE MIGHTY FORTRESS
LOOSEJAW THE NIGHTMARE FISH

OUT IN AUGUST 2016!

Don't miss the
BRAND NEW
Special Bumper Edition:

REPTA
THE SPIKED BRUTE

OUT IN JUNE 2016

WIN AN EXCLUSIVE
GOODY BAG

In every Sea Quest book the Sea Quest logo is
hidden in one of the pictures. Find the logos in books
25-28, make a note of which pages they appear on and
go online to enter the competition at

www.seaquestbooks.co.uk

Each month we will put all of the correct entries into a draw
and select one winner to receive a special Sea Quest goody bag.

You can also send your entry on a postcard to:

Sea Quest Competition, Orchard Books,
Carmelite House, 50 Victoria Embankment,
London, EC4Y 0DZ

Don't forget to include your name and address!

GOOD LUCK

Closing Date: May 31st 2016

Competition open to UK and Republic of Ireland residents. No purchase required.
For full terms and conditions please see www.seaquestbooks.co.uk

DARE YOU DIVE IN?

Deep in the water lurks
a new breed of Beast.

If you want the latest news and
exclusive Sea Quest goodies, join our
Sea Quest Club!

Visit www.seaquestbooks.co.uk/club
and sign up today!

IF YOU LIKE SEA QUEST,
YOU'LL LOVE BEAST QUEST!

Series 1: COLLECT THEM ALL!

An evil wizard has enchanted the magical beasts of Avantia. Only a true hero can free the beasts and save the land. Is Tom the hero Avantia has been waiting for?

978 1 84616 483 5

978 1 84616 482 8

978 1 84616 484 2

978 1 84616 486 6

978 1 84616 485 9

978 1 84616 487 3

DON'T MISS THE
BRAND NEW SERIES OF:

Series 16: THE SIEGE OF GWILDOR

STYRO
THE SNAPPING BRUTE

978 1 40833 986 2

RONAK
THE TOXIC TERROR

978 1 40833 996 1

SOLIX
THE DEADLY SWARM

978 1 40833 988 6

KANIS
THE SHADOW HOUND

978 1 40833 994 7

COMING SOON